JACK TAR

JACK TAR

Written by
JEAN RUSSELL LARSON

Illustrated by
MERCER MAYER

Macrae Smith Company · *Philadelphia*

Library of Congress Catalog Card Number LC 72-87983
Manufactured in the United States of America

Trade SBN: 8255-5200-1
Library Edition SBN: 8255-5201-x

6903

There was once a young Northumbrian lad; Jack Wookey was his name. He tramped from Flodden to Liverpool, for he had decided to go to sea. There he shipped aboard the *Begum of Bengal*, bound for India.

The captain of the great ship was square-jawed Mr. Beeston, whose mission in life was to perfect the character of those lads entrusted to his care. From dawn until long past dark, his kindly voice rang out across the bow of the *Begum:* "Secure the mainsail, you wooden-headed sons of a jellyfish! Hoist the jib or you'll walk the plank."

Because Jack Wookey was an industrious young man, he rose quickly to a position of trust. He was allowed the privilege of serving meals to Mr. Beeston in the latter's cabin. He would lay the snowy linens and set out the Wedgwood teapot and the Sheffield tray. Then he would stand silently by as Mr. Beeston fell to, devouring everything in sight.

1

Things went beautifully for some time and doubtless would have continued so, but one day Jack made a serious mistake. It was while he was serving elevenses, Assam tea and clootie puddin', that the disaster occurred.

"Sugar, sir," Jack said, extending the decorated tin which, unknown to him, had become a repository for the epsom salts in which the cook soaked his aching feet.

Captain Beeston scooped the white crystals into his tea, stirred briskly and then drank deeply.

"*Awp*," he cried, gasping. "What is in this tea?"

Jack's eyes widened. "I brewed it myself, sir," he croaked, "exactly as I always do."

Captain Beeston examined the tea, then turned and inspected the contents of the sugar tin.

"Salts!" he bellowed, leaping up from his chair. "You've fed me salts, you simpleton. You have failed at your post of duty. You've dishonored your profession. I'll have your hide for this!"

Jack was clapped into irons, and when at last the *Begum of Bengal* docked in Bombay, the unfortunate young man was sent from the ship in disgrace. He slunk down the gangplank to the catcalls and jeers of his fellow seamen and lost himself in the hurly-burly of the dusty street.

For three days Jack wandered the city, loathing himself for what he had done and for what he had become, an outcast. But no life is all shadows, and on the fourth day of his exile Jack chanced to overhear a piece of news that was to alter the entire course of his life. It seemed that the British Resident in Bombay had been the victim of a theft. A priceless necklace of black pearls, which had been entrusted to the Resident's care by the Maharajah of Manipur, and which the Resident was to deliver to Her Majesty the Queen upon her forthcoming visit to India, had been pilfered from the Government House. It was rumored that a certain seaman from the *Begum of Bengal*, Mick Muxlow by name, had vanished along with the pearls and was believed by one and all to be the thief.

"Now here's a piece of luck," Jack said to himself, when he had heard the news. "All I need to do is capture Mick Muxlow and recover the pearls in order to redeem myself. Nothing could be simpler."

Because he had come from a good home in which traditions were respected, Jack knew that the first duty of an Englishman in a foreign port was to pay a call at the British Government House. He now rebuked himself for having postponed that call three days.

"I will mix duty with business," he decided. "I will learn what I can about the theft of the pearls. Somehow or other I must pick up Mick Muxlow's trail, and the Government House is a likely place for doing it."

He hastened at once to the Government House and presented himself. A young man in a stiff collar and black coat led him into a large, shuttered room where the Resident sat hunched over his desk. Overhead a fan whirred softly. Two cut-glass decanters were on a silver tray at his side, as well as several pieces of crystal marked with regimental emblems. Jack was impressed.

"Lord Lummox . . ." the young man in the black coat said, coughing softly.

"What is it, Pippin-Fry?" the Resident asked, looking up from his work.

"Mr. Wookey is calling" Pippin-Fry announced. "Will you want tea served?"

Lord Lummox looked startled, then narrowed his eyes as he regarded Jack's seaman's garb.

"You would be Jack Wookey?" he asked levelly.

"The same," Jack admitted.

Pippin-Fry shrank back in horror.

"The same who disgraced himself on the *Begum of Bengal?*" Lord Lummox pressed on.

Jack swallowed hard.

"I've come to pay my respects," he croaked nervously, "and to learn what I can about the theft of the black pearls. Will you acquaint me with the facts?"

"Not likely!" Pippin-Fry cried.

"See here," Lord Lummox said, rising, "we aren't running a club for beachcombers and amateur detectives. You have a nerve showing your face here after you disgraced yourself in the service of one of our finest ships."

"But I want to locate those pearls," Jack explained.

"Colonel Frobisher has directed that the entire British army comb India for that necklace," Lord Lummox snapped, "and you are not to interfere in the matter. Is that clear? Now you had better go."

Jack slumped visibly.

"Where will I go?" he asked. "What will I do?"

"It would be best," Lord Lummox said in a kindlier tone, "if you dropped out of sight altogether. You must have a family. Consider them. How much better it would be if they could forget you had ever existed."

Jack nodded, thinking of his mother and father in England and wondering how long it would be before the story of his ruin reached their ears. Then he straightened his shoulders and thrust out his chin defiantly.

"I mean to redeem myself," he said firmly. "I am going to make amends for what I have done, and one day I will have tea in this very room with you; wait and see!"

"Plucky chap," Lord Lummox muttered as he watched Jack go down the wide walk between the banyan trees and enter the city street once more. Pippin-Fry nodded, then resumed his work.

There was nothing for Jack to do but wander the city, stopping here and there to inquire if a tall, red-haired seaman had been noticed passing by. Everywhere he received the same answer. No one had seen Mick Muxlow. Once Jack thought he himself saw Mick Muxlow at the far end of a narrow street in the Bazaar of the silk merchants, but before he could push his way through the crowd of shoppers, the man had vanished.

Toward evening, as Jack walked forlornly at the edge of the city, an old woman went past him down the road in a lumbering cart drawn by a bullock. He was about to raise his voice in salute when to his astonishment the old woman, cart, bullock and all seemed to vanish into the side of a steep hill near the road. He stopped short and rubbed his eyes, straining to see in the gathering twilight.

"I say," he murmured, "that is odd. I'll just go and have a look-see."

He approached the hill, moving as quietly as he could. Peering through the scraggly trees and the tall withered grass, he saw the mouth of a cave.

"So that's where she went," he whispered aloud.

Going closer in order to peer into the opening, Jack stumbled over the gnarled root of a tree and sprawled headlong onto the floor of the cave.

"What's this?" a startled voice cried, and Jack looked up to see the old woman standing above him, a lighted lamp in her hand.

"I'm dreadfully sorry, madam," Jack said, leaping up and brushing himself off. "I had no intention of bursting into your cave that way. I was only——"

"Spying!" the old woman cried. "That was what you were doing. You're a sneak!"

Jack hung his head in shame. Was there no depth to which he would not sink?"

"If you will allow me to explain," he pleaded, "you will soon see that I am in desperate straits."

The old woman regarded him suspiciously.

"Well," she said at last, "I will hear your story. But it had better be a good one."

Starting at the beginning, Jack told his story. How he had set out from Flodden with high hopes and had ended in deepest disgrace, unwelcome even at his own government house. Then he set forth his plan for redeeming himself—for capturing Mick Muxlow and regaining the precious black pearls.

The old woman listened in silence.

"It is lucky for you that you met me," she said, when he had finished. "If anyone knows anything about stolen merchandise, I know about it. I just happen to be the most infamous desperado in all of Bombay!"

"Desperado!" Jack cried. "You?"

The old woman scowled at him.

"What is so strange about that?" she snapped. "I will have you know that the mention of my name strikes fear in the hearts of people hereabout."

Jack was astonished. There was nothing about the old woman to suggest that she was dangerous. In fact she looked quite comical, with her hair straggling about her face and her shoulders swathed in shawls.

"Who are you," Jack inquired, "and precisely what is your business?"

"My name is Tootie," the old woman answered. "I steal from the poor and sell to the rich." She cackled with laughter.

Jack recoiled from her as from a snake. Here was a flagrant flaunting of tradition, and all of his finer senses were affronted. He could scarcely bear the sight of the old woman now. How low he had fallen, to commerce with such as this!

"Oh," Tootie cooed, "I have shocked you. What a sheltered life you have led. But now you are no better than I, and you had better get used to the idea."

Jack shuddered.

"Please," he begged, knowing he had no choice but to deal with the woman, "tell me what you can about Mick Muxlow and the stolen pearls."

Old Tootie cackled again.

"Just before I started out from Bombay this afternoon to come here—this is my country house (all of the better people have them, you know)—well, just before I started out, a tall, red-haired seaman came to me with a string of black pearls.

8

" 'I can let you have them cheap,' says he.

" 'I'll not touch them with a barge pole,' says I, 'for the British are combing Bombay for them.' "

"Then you didn't purchase the pearls?" Jack asked, disappointed.

"I didn't," old Tootie said, "but I know where that seaman went with them. I sent him north, to Delhi. There is a woman there who will take a chance on anything. Her name is Ram. She operates a sweet shop."

So Mick Muxlow had been in Bombay until an hour or so before—and his plans were an open secret! Jack was overjoyed.

"Before you leave here to follow the red-haired seaman," Tootie said, "there is something I must tell you. Because I am a gypsy I am able to foretell the future, and yours is not a bright and shiny one."

"I put no faith in prophecy," Jack declared stoutly. "There is no scientific evidence to suggest that —— "

Tootie groaned.

"If you scorn a gypsy's warning," she cautioned, "it will go doubly hard for you! I foresee a difficult road before you, and I also foresee that we will meet again, you and I."

"Do you really believe that?" Jack asked sarcastically.

The gypsy laughed. "I can practically guarantee it," she said.

"I am in your debt for the information concerning Mick Muxlow," Jack admitted. "How can I repay you?"

Tootie smiled wickedly.

"Don't trouble yourself about that," she said. "You have already repaid me handsomely."

Jack went away, musing over the strange remark. Indeed, the full meaning of it did not become clear to him until he was well on the road north and discovered that his gold pocket watch was missing.

Darkness fell, and Jack trudged on. He was growing very hungry, for he had not eaten that day. Captain Beeston had not seen fit to grant severance pay, and Jack's final shilling had been spent for bread and figs on the previous day.

Jack lay down at the side of the road and rested for a time, attempting to push from his mind thoughts of dropped scones and bannocks dripping butter. But soon he was up again, pressing forward toward Delhi with determination.

At dawn, a cart drawn by a bullock came rumbling down the road and Jack prevailed upon the driver, a small, wizened man, to give him a ride. Since the old man said little and Jack was left to his thoughts, he fell to planning the manner in which he would deliver the pearls, when recovered, to the Queen herself. In all likelihood he would be knighted and sent into Parliament, where he would distinguish himself. In his mind's eye he saw the furor he would cause as he rose to speak out on a major issue; the respectful way in which younger members of Parliament would defer to his every utterance.

"That's Old Wookey, don't you know," they would whisper. "He's the chappie who gave the Prime Minister the mitten for talking out of turn."

The cart jolted to a stop suddenly in a small village, and

Jack understood from the old driver's gestures that his ride had come to an end.

A crowd of villagers gathered as Jack descended from the cart.

"Have you such a thing as an inn about?" Jack inquired, preparing to ask credit on the purchase of a bun and tea.

The villagers only stared at the young man, their eyes narrowed.

"Perhaps my bearing dazzles them," Jack mused. "A British tar is a splendid specimen and the backbone of the Empire! I must strive to put them at their ease, since obviously they are in awe of me."

He stretched out a hand, palm upward, then brought his fingers toward his mouth, indicating that he wished to dine.

"Thief!" shrieked one of the villagers.

"Thief!" echoed all of the others, pointing accusing fingers at Jack.

They fell upon the poor young man and began pummeling him with their fists. With great difficulty Jack managed to extricate himself from the melee, leaving the frenzied villagers to clout and pound one another. Smoothing his uniform, Jack walked with all the dignity he could muster to where the old cart driver stood, apart from the fracas.

"I say," Jack remarked, attempting a hearty voice, "that was awfully disagreeable."

The old man shrugged to show he had no interest in the proceedings.

"There he is," a woman screeched, disentangling herself

from the knot of villagers and pointing to Jack.

"Wait," Jack said, raising a hand to half the throng as it prepared to descend upon him once more. "At least tell me what crime I have committed."

"Not you, but one like you," an old woman shouted. "Just yesterday at sunset another of your kind, a red-haired seaman, arrived in this village, and when he left not a scrap of food remained. He pleaded hunger, and we extended hospitality. He began with the figs, devoured the rice, gobbled the seed cakes, and swallowed up all the fruit that we brought him. Oh, he was a terrible pig! And now you come to clean up anything he left. But we will clean you up instead!"

The villagers advanced menacingly toward Jack, who smiled a smile of loving charity.

"Good people" he said sweetly, "you have nothing to fear from me. I would not touch one morsel that has not been freely given; and as for the man of whom you speak, he is a hunted criminal. At this very moment I am on his

trail, intending to deliver him and his ill-gotten goods to the Queen."

The villagers halted in their tracks, impressed by Jack's words.

"That blighter Mick Muxlow," Jack continued, "is no fit representative of Her Majesty's navy." Jack suddenly blushed, remembering his own disgrace and questionable status. Then, however, he straightened his shoulders, recalling his resolve to redeem himself. "Now with your permission, I will bid you all farewell and be away on my errand."

"Not until you have eaten," a man shouted. "We will comb the village and surrounding countryside until we have found food for you, so that we may demonstrate our regret for dealing so unfairly with you."

When Jack left the village two hours later, he had dined well. There had been golden yams, and an orange, and barley sugar. He thought of the villagers with warmth.

For days Jack traveled, sometimes walking, sometimes, riding in rickety, swaying carts. Day and night he strained his eyes, watching to catch a glimpse of Mick Muxlow ahead on the road. He wondered if Mick Muxlow was catching rides in carts too, and supposed that he must be, since the distance between the two of them never seemed to close.

At length, weary and on foot, Jack approached the outskirts of Delhi. He could see already the bustle in the streets, and he realized with despair that it would be difficult if not impossible to locate Mick Muxlow in such a throng.

At the edge of the city, in the shade of a thorn tree, sat three Chinese gentlemen who obviously had a problem as great as Jack's own, for their chins rested in their hands and their faces wore woebegone expressions. They were clad in traditional robes of yellow silk.

"Beastly hot!" Jack observed cheerily, approaching the three gentlemen.

They glanced up at him, nodded, then resumed their downcast attitudes.

"See here," Jack cried heartily, "you fellows seem so melancholy. Things can't really be as bad as all that. Give us a smile now."

One of the gentlemen looked up at Jack and sneered.

"Little you know about it," he snapped. "We are the Wong Brothers!"

Jack pondered that declaration for several moments. From the gentleman's tone it was obvious that the name Wong should explain the gloom of the three, but the fact was that the name meant nothing whatever to Jack.

"I am afraid you will need to explain further" Jack said, trying his best to be diplomatic. "The name of Wong is unfamiliar to me."

The three gentlemen regarded him with stunned silence. At last one of them spoke.

"We are tumblers," he explained. "Odd that you have never heard of us, since we are world-famous."

"Oh, I'm sure of it!" Jack cried hastily. "But since you are such a success in your chosen profession, why are you so miserable? And why are you sitting here at the edge of the city?"

The three groaned in unison.

"The trouble is," one of them explained, "that there are four Wong Brothers."

"Where is the fourth?" Jack inquired, looking around.

"That's just it," the tumbler replied. "He has left us to become a fish peddler. He claims it will be a position of security in his old age, when he is no longer able to tumble."

Jack rubbed his chin thoughtfully.

"I still don't see—" he began.

"Our problem?" the tumbler cried. "It is simple. We are now only three—a three-cornered tumbling act. The

world is filled with three-cornered tumbling acts. We have no fourth man to stand atop the pyramid, and we are scheduled to perform in Delhi this very day. We will be laughed out of the city."

Jack thought about that. It was the duty of a British seaman, even an unemployed one, to assist those less fortunate than himself.

"See here," he said at last, "perhaps I could join your act for one performance."

The three tumblers seemed startled.

"Do you mean it?" one of them cried.

"Have you any experience?" another demanded.

Jack said that he did indeed mean it, and that although he had no experience whatever, he hoped to make up in determination what he lacked in skill.

"Perhaps you have a natural gift for tumbling," one of the tumblers said. "Tell me, have you an index finger on your left hand which is an eighth-inch longer than that on your right hand?"

16

"Why yes," Jack cried. "How did you know?"

"And has that index finger a nail with a perfect half moon?" the tumbler continued.

"Yes, yes!" Jack cried.

"And on that half moon," the tumbler whispered confidentially, "is there a small silver mark?"

"Yes," Jack cried, "there is!"

"Then you are no tumbler," the Chinese gentleman said morosely, "for a true tumbler never has such a finger."

Jack pursed his lips, puzzled.

"Let us waste no more time," one of the Wong brothers said, "for I am growing hungry and we shall not be able to eat until we have been paid for the performance."

Jack and the three tumblers entered the city and made their way through the crowds of shoppers. At length they reached the wide space in the shadow of Jama Masjid, the Great Mosque. There they halted, and the eldest of the Wong brothers called for the attention of passersby and merchants alike.

"You see before you," he cried, "the world famous Wong brothers, tumblers extraordinary. It will be our pleasure to perform for you now, and your pleasure to watch us."

Shoppers and merchants alike stood in awed silence, watching in hushed expectation.

"Since one of our brothers has left the act," the tumbler continued, "we are featuring a guest artist today. I have the honor to present—" He turned to Jack. "What is your name?" he whispered.

"Jack Wookey," Jack replied.

"I have the honor to present Jack Wookey," the tumbler announced. "Now behold the finest tumbling act in the world!"

With that the three Wong brothers began a series of somersaults both forward and backward, headstands, and cartwheels.

The crowd cheered wildly, and small girls threw rose petals.

"When do I perform?" Jack asked as one of the brothers executed a headstand.

"Your turn will come," the tumbler replied.

For some time the three cavorted, their faces flushed with success and wreathed in smiles. At last the eldest motioned for Jack to join them.

"This is the finale," the tumbler whispered. "It is the specialty that has brought us fame. Just follow our lead."

He and another of the tumblers set themselves in the center of the street, hands on hips. The third tumbler, standing some distance from the other two, appeared to size up the situation, then darted forward and with a flying leap landed astride the shoulders of his brothers.

The crowd went wild; then a hushed silence fell upon them. They turned and stared at Jack.

In that split second Jack saw what was expected of him, and he was terror-stricken. Suffering as he did from a fear of heights, he had scrupulously avoided all ladders, crows-nests, and balconies.

He had no idea what the world looked like from the top of a Chinese human pyramid, but instinct told him it was too monstrous for words!

18

He shook his head, indicating he had no intention of ascending the triangle. The crowd hissed, and the Wong brothers scowled menacingly.

Jack reconsidered. The performance would soon be over, for he had been assured this was the finale. Then there would be pay and food. Jack was exceedingly hungry.

Backing away from the pyramid and drawing in his breath, Jack took a running jump and landed, miraculously, atop the shoulders of the third Wong brother. Once again the crowd went wild and the air was filled with raining flower petals.

Jack swayed dangerously to and fro but managed to place his hands on his hips in a debonair manner. He squeezed his eyes tight shut to avoid witnessing his own fall. Then, since he seemed secure after all, he opened them and glanced cautiously about. The sun was shining and everything appeared as it had before, only farther beneath him. He breathed a deep sigh of relief and accomplishment.

Suddenly, at the edge of the crowd, Jack caught sight of a mop of tousled red hair. Shading his eyes with one hand, he picked out the face of Mick Muxlow beneath the hair. Jack gasped.

"Stand still up there!" one of the tumblers cried.

Jack teetered, struggling to maintain his balance in the excitement.

"See here," he cried, "I must come down at once!"

"What's that you say?" the tumbler directly beneath him demanded.

19

"I must come down," Jack shouted.

He shaded his eyes once more and caught sight of Mick Muxlow, retreating up a narrow street away from the throng.

In one desperate effort to loose his ankles from the grip of the tumbler beneath him, Jack jiggled violently up and down. But he lost his balance and fell backward, upsetting the entire pyramid. The crowd howled with laughter.

Scarcely waiting until his feet touched the street, Jack set out on a dead run to overtake Mick Muxlow.

"Scoundrel!" the Wong brothers shrieked. "Rogue!" "We will not rest until we have taught you a lesson! You have ruined our reputation."

Jack heard their running feet behind him and turned to see them overtaking him, their eyes blazing with anger. How quickly the pursuer had become the pursued! Jack could not be sure what the tumblers would do to him if they should catch him, but he was certain it would be unpleasant. He quickened his steps and slid round a corner into a dark alley. Just as the sound of the approaching tumblers reached his ears, Jack's groping hands touched a doorway in the wall of the alley. Pushing open that door, he slipped inside and closed it quickly behind him.

Inside, the light was blinding after the darkness of the alley. Jack blinked his eyes.

"What ho!" a voice, unmistakably British, boomed.

"What ho!" Jack replied uncertainly, his eyes slowly becoming accustomed to the light. A large man clad in white stood before him, surrounded by gleaming pots and pans.

"What ho!" the large man repeated, obviously awaiting an explanation of Jack's presence there.

Jack cleared his throat nervously.

"Awfully glad to see you," he said chirpily. "I am escaping from a troupe of Chinese acrobats. Would you be so good as to tell me where I am?"

"You are in the kitchen of the Empire Hotel," the large man bellowed, his face growing red, "and I am the head chef!"

"The Empire Hotel?" Jack cried. "I say, that's topping! Isn't this the hotel which Lord Cranshaw prefers when in India?"

"His Lordship has never confided in me," the chef replied acidly. "Now, if you have quite finished escaping from the Chinese acrobats, would you kindly leave my kitchen?"

Jack thought for a moment.

"I was wondering," he said at last, "if I might have a spot of lunch before I leave. This was to be payday, but an unforeseen circumstance has arisen and I find myself without a bob."

The chef glowered at Jack.

"I will feed you," he snapped, "if you will work for your meal. An important party is due to arrive momentarily and one of the waiters is ill. If you will serve the roast beef, I will give you lunch."

"It's a bargain," Jack declared heartily. "Lead me to it."

After washing up, Jack donned a waiter's jacket and watched as the chef placed the mammoth roast of beef on a serving cart. Its outside was golden brown and crisp, while its inside, exposed at one end, was a beautiful shade of pink. Jack felt faint at the sight of it. Alongside the roast were the implements with which he was to carve it, and he longed to begin, to see the juices trickle from the meat.

"The party has entered the dining room," the chef announced, "and has begun on the soup. Stand ready."

"Aye, aye, sir," Jack snapped, standing at attention.

After several minutes the chef signaled for Jack to enter

the dining room with his precious cargo. Trundling the cart before him, Jack smiled broadly and scanned the dining room, searching for the party he was to serve. The tables, which were positioned about the room, were ringed with diners in a festive mood. Laughter and the buzz of pleasant conversation filled the air. After a moment, Jack's glance came to rest on a table at the far end of the room, and his heart leaped to his throat.

"Lord Lummox!" he gasped. "And Mr. Pippin-Fry!"

"Psst! Over there," another waiter hissed in Jack's ear. He indicated the table at which Lord Lummox and Pippin-Fry sat. "There's the place for your roast beef."

Jack groaned. He wanted lunch badly, and would have some just as soon as he served the roast beef, but in the meantime Lord Lummox might cause a terrible scene upon seeing him and then he would be tossed back into the alley with no lunch at all.

Suddenly an idea occurred to him. Edging close to an empty table, Jack slid the white linen cloth from it and enveloped himself, mummylike, in it. Then he grasped the serving cart and sped to Lord Lummox's table, crooning shrilly.

"Ah there," Lord Lummox cried jovially, when he spied the roast beef.

Jack pressed a corner of the tablecloth to his face with one hand and took up the carving knife with the other hand, attacking the meat with a vengeance.

"My good man," Lord Lummox cried, "take care! What we want are thin slices." He held his forefinger and thumb close together to indicate a paper-thin width.

Jack hummed on in a high, hysterical voice, sawing furiously at the meat.

"This will never do," Pippin-Fry objected. "Do leave off that hacking at once!"

Jack's voice rose to new heights and his carving became even more frenzied, for he realized he must make an exit soon or be discovered. All eyes in the dining room were now turned toward him.

"I demand to know why you are singing," Lord Lummox roared, rising from his chair.

"Lullaby," Jack croaked gruffly, attempting to disguise his voice.

"Lullaby to whom?" Pippin-Fry cried.

Jack nodded to the beef roast with his head.

24

"To that," he rasped.

The room rocked with laughter. Pippin-Fry stared open-mouthed at Jack, who was backing from the table, his tablecloth clutched tightly about him. All thoughts of lunch had fled from the mind of the young seaman, and his only desire was to escape from the hotel.

"What is the trouble here?" the chef demanded, appearing suddenly at Jack's side. "I am a temperamental man and I will have no disturbance distracting attention from my food!"

Leaning close to peer into the eyes that stared out from the tablecloth shroud, the chef inadvertently stepped upon a trailing corner, so that as Jack backed away, the cloth unwound and he stood revealed before the entire company.

"You!" Lord Lummox spluttered, pointing an accusing finger at Jack. "Didn't you wreak havoc enough in the Royal Navy? Must you dog my footsteps and trample that sacred emblem of the Empire, roast beef?"

Jack struggled manfully for words, but finding none that suited the occasion, he turned and fled from the dining room, pursued by Lord Lummox and Pippin-Fry. As he passed through the kitchen on his way to the alley, a mess boy who had heard the uproar and pitied Jack managed to pass the unfortunate young man two Bath buns and a slice of suet pudding.

"Stout work!" Jack cried breathlessly, snatching the provender.

"Leg it, old dear," the mess boy shouted. "They're gaining on you!"

Jack did not look back until he was into the alley and around the corner. Then, seeing no one behind him, he leaned against a wall and devoured one of the buns.

"This is a fine kettle of herring," Jack groaned. "I can't hope to find Mick Muxlow, for at any moment I may be snatched up by the Chinese acrobats or Lord Lummox and company." A sudden thought struck him. "Here's an idea," he cried aloud. "If I were to assume a disguise—a clever one and not just an ordinary tablecloth—then I could escape my pursuers and come upon Muxlow unaware." He hugged himself with happiness, then made of the remaining Bath bun two cheerful mouthfuls.

Proceeding furtively into the street, Jack exchanged the slice of suet pudding for a tattered dhoti and a striped turban that had seen better days. The young man with whom Jack made the deal went away bareheaded, his long shirt whipping about his thin legs, munching the pudding.

It was the work of only a moment for Jack to clothe himself in the Indian garb and be off down the street. He was very tired and decided to secure accommodations before night fell. Several days of searching might lie ahead. Since he had no money, lodging presented a problem.

Through the streets Jack walked, stepping gingerly out of the way as people on bicycles sped past. An astrologer clutched at his sleeve, threatening to call the fates down upon Jack's luckless head if the young man did not pay to have his future revealed. Thin, high-pitched sounds filled his ears, and Jack found himself swaying in time with the music of flutes and stringed instruments. But still he had not found a place to lay his head when night came.

As the sun set and all the air was still, Jack halted before a small, shabby hotel. He surveyed the building for a moment, straightened his turban, and went inside.

"How may I serve you?" the man inside cried, hurrying forward to greet Jack. "Your wish is my command."

"The fact is," Jack said, "you can do something for me. I am in need of lodging, but I have no money with which to pay you."

"In that case," the man said, haughtily, "why don't you sleep in the street?"

"My good man!" Jack cried. "What a monstrous thing to suggest."

His horrified manner took the proprietor by surprise and he stammered a hasty apology for having insulted Jack.

"Now then," Jack said, "shall we resume our business? Perhaps there is a bit of work I can do in exchange for a bed."

The proprietor seemed to consider briefly.

"I have it," he said. "Only today I engaged the services of a man to clean the stairs and the entryway and to carry out the rubbish. Since he has no money, I am providing him with a room in exchange for his work. And since he claims to have business with local merchants in the daytime, he will do his work here at night, sleeping in the room for a few hours after daybreak."

"That is a very fine arrangement," Jack said, "but what has it to do with me?"

"It occurs to me," the proprietor explained, "that you might sleep in that room at night, while the other occupant is at work. Then you could arise at daybreak and work in the kitchen, scrubbing pots and pans. How does that strike you?"

Jack thought for a moment.

"Would I have most of the day free?" he asked.

"Yes, you will be able to do as you like, just as soon as all of the pots and pans are cleaned. Have you business in the city too?"

Jack smiled.

"As a matter of fact, I have," he said.

"I wish you success," the proprietor said. "Now I will show you to your room. The other occupant should be leaving it now to come downstairs and work."

The proprietor led the way to the shadowy stairs, and Jack followed. Halfway up, they met a man wrapped in a loose-fitting hooded cloak.

"This is the man who will occupy your room during the morning while you are at work," the proprietor said.

The man on the stairs bowed to Jack.

"My name is Punji," Jack said. It had occurred to him suddenly that a false name would be a help in concealing his true identity.

"My name is Ponji," the man on the stairs declared.

"What an extraordinary coincidence," the hotel proprietor remarked.

The man called Ponji descended the stairs, and Jack followed the proprietor upward until they reached the second floor and a small, dimly lighted room.

"Sleep well," the proprietor said, "and be on time for work in the morning. Mr. Ponji will be wanting the room at daybreak."

Jack lay down and in nearly no time was asleep.

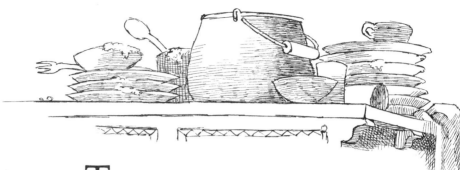

The next morning, as Jack was dreaming for the fourth time that the chef at the Empire Hotel had bundled him into an egg roll and was serving him up to the Wong brothers and Lord Lummox, a knock sounded at the door. Jack arose, donned his turban and opened the door to find Mr. Ponji standing in the passageway. As on the previous night, Mr. Ponji's hooded robe was drawn tightly about him.

"Come in," Jack said, stepping aside.

Mr. Ponji streamed into the room and nestled on the bed without a word. Jack was content to go away without conversation.

Only one pot in the shabby hotel kitchen was clean, and Jack was so discouraged by the sight of the towering pile of dirty ones that he flung the clean one into the heap.

"May as well wash them all," he sighed. "I won't be done until noon, and at this very moment Mick Muxlow is probably exchanging the pearls for money at the shop of Ram."

When at last all of the pots and pans had been scrubbed clean, Jack removed the apron that covered his dhoti and sped from the kitchen. At the front door he nearly collided with Mr. Ponji, who was also leaving the hotel.

"After you," Jack said, stepping aside to allow Mr. Ponji to precede him through the door.

Mr. Ponji bowed low and walked out into the sunshine, drawing his cloak more closely about him.

"Hmm," Jack said aloud. "Quiet chap. I wonder just what business he has in the city and where he comes from."

There was no time to be wasted. Jack asked directions of a passing peddler and was soon on his way to the shop of Ram, the woman whom the gypsy had recommended to Mick Muxlow.

The sun had already described half its gigantic arc and was directly overhead. Jack resolved that before it set in the west he would have collared Muxlow and be in possession of the black pearls. Down Chandni Chauk, the "Silver Street," hurried Jack. Carts rumbled past him, and the din of moneylenders' raucous cries filled his ears. The hotel proprietor had thoughtfully provided Jack with a bite of breakfast, but the scents of brewing tea and sun-ripened fruit were inviting.

The sweet shop of Ram was a tumbledown building set back from the street. The doorway was small, and Jack needed to stoop to enter. The interior of the shop was dimly lighted.

"What do you want here?" a sharp voice snapped.

Jack looked around but saw no one.

"I would like to talk with Ram," Jack said uncertainly.

"Who are you?" the voice demanded.

Once more Jack looked around him but saw no one.

"I would prefer not to reveal my identity," he said, addressing a large jade vase that sat in a corner. Someone had to be in the shop, but for the life of him Jack was unable to discern where that voice came from.

Suddenly, in the dim light of the flickering lamp that sat next to the vase, a stooped figure stepped into view, muffled in a shawl.

"There is no need to tell me who you are," the figure said, cackling with laughter. "I have recognized you."

"And I you!" Jack cried in astonishment. "You are Tootie the gypsy!"

The gypsy waggled her finger at Jack.

"Ah, ah," she corrected, "now I am Ram, proprietor of this shop."

Jack stared at her, open-mouthed.

"I see that you are surprised," the gypsy said. "Allow me to explain."

"Please do," Jack urged.

The gypsy sat down upon a rug and motioned for Jack to be seated opposite her.

"Since I am an enterprising woman," she began, "and since my business in Bombay was flourishing, I decided some time ago to open a branch store here in Delhi. I am pleased to report that I am prospering here also."

"But why did you tell Mick Muxlow to come here with the stolen pearls?" Jack demanded. "Why didn't you purchase them in Bombay and be done with the matter?"

The gypsy leaned close to Jack.

"I told him to come here," she replied in a furtive whisper, "because I purchase items in Delhi that I would not dare to touch in Bombay, if you see what I mean."

Jack thought that he did.

"Unfortunately," the gypsy continued, "I did not even dare purchase those black pearls in this city. While I was en route here I learned that the British authorities were closing in fast."

"Do you mean to say that you have seen Mick Muxlow in Delhi," Jack cried, "and that he offered you the pearls again?"

"He was here," the gypsy replied, "yesterday. I refused the pearls and sent him on his way."

Jack thought for a long moment, attempting to make sense of all the gypsy had said.

"But why did you tell me Mick Muxlow and the pearls would be here, in Delhi?" he asked at last. "You knew I was after those pearls."

The gypsy laughed slyly.

"I intended to let you have them, for a price," she explained, "but I could not be sure how soon you would arrive, and in the meantime the British authorities might have swooped down upon me and found me with stolen goods. I could not risk it."

Jack sighed. He had been so sure that the end of the road lay at the shop of Ram. Now he had no idea where to search for Mick Muxlow, and in addition there was the disturbing news that the British were combing Delhi at that very moment, searching for the pearls. Suppose some enterprising young officer should find Muxlow before he, Jack, could. Then all hope of reclaiming his lost honor would be gone.

"Have you any idea where Mick Muxlow may have gone?" Jack asked.

"Not the slightest," the gypsy admitted. "My interest in the matter has ended, since no profit is involved."

"That's all jolly well for you," Jack said, "but what about me? If I don't recover those pearls, I'll remain an outcast forever. You might at least offer to help me."

The gypsy seemed genuinely shocked.

"Help you?" she cried. "Do an act of kindness and ruin my reputation? What can you be thinking of?"

"No one need ever know," Jack assured her. "Dear old gypsy, remember our friendship."

"Friendship?" the gypsy screeched. "I've only met you once before!"

Jack regretted the necessity of asking help of the woman, for he had not forgotten that she was a criminal of the worst sort, but his situation was a desperate one.

"But we were together in Bombay," he reminded her. "Dear old Bombay! Perhaps you could use your gypsy powers to assist me."

"Ah ha!" the gypsy cried scornfully. "So you do believe in my gypsy powers, after all."

Jack shook his head stubbornly.

"I do not believe in them," he declared firmly, "but neither do I disbelieve. Mine is an open mind. Prove to me that you have such gifts by helping me to gain possession of the pearls."

The gypsy was silent for several moments, obviously considering Jack's challenge.

"Very well," she said at last, "I will help you. But you must promise that no one will ever know. If it were ever learned that I had done a good deed I would not be able to hold up my head in public."

It occurred to Jack to press for the return of his gold watch, which he was certain the gypsy had pinched, but he decided against offending his newly won ally.

The two fell to planning how they might find Mick Muxlow, and at length it was decided that Jack would search Chandni Chauk while the gypsy would explore its offshoots, inquiring of her various friends whether they had seen the red-haired seaman.

"What do your mystic powers have to say concerning Mick's whereabouts?" Jack asked.

"The stars are not in an auspicious position for prophecy at this moment," the gypsy said haughtily. "When you are in truly desperate straits, just when you need help the most, then my second sight will come to your rescue. In the meantime, we will search for the desperado and meet here at my shop tomorrow to compare results."

Jack rose from the rug and straightened his turban.

"Very well," he agreed. "And if either of us should locate Mick before that time, a message must be sent round to the other. I'm stopping at the Raja Hotel."

For the remainder of the day Jack wandered the street, straining his eyes for a glimpse of Mick Muxlow and inquiring of merchants whether they had done business with the seaman. The roadway was crowded with traders from far-off lands, saffron-robed Hindus, and bearded Moslems.

"This is a frightfully busy place," Jack observed, "and it would be easier to locate Muxlow in a freighter laden with red-haired seamen. But a British tar does not give in, so the motto is 'Carry on'! I'll return to the hotel now, and perhaps there will be a message from the gypsy waiting for me."

But there was no message waiting, and Jack went off to bed, weary and troubled. Perhaps the British officials had already taken Muxlow into custody and at that very moment were gloating over the recovered pearls. In which case he, Jack, would roam foreign shores for the remainder of his life, a man without a country.

The next morning, as on the previous morning, Jack was awakened by a knock at his door. He rose and admitted Mr. Ponji, his mysterious roommate, then sped downstairs to the kitchen to attack the pots and pans. The sooner his work was done, the sooner he would be off to the shop of the gypsy to learn if she had news for him.

As Jack entered the kitchen, he realized that he had forgotten his apron, and so he returned to his room to get it. Realizing that Mr. Ponji would probably be asleep, Jack stole quietly into the room and was about to pick up the apron when he was startled to hear Mr. Ponji's voice.

"I believe he is talking in his sleep," Jack mused. "Poor chap must be worn out from cleaning."

"Pearls," Mr. Ponji mumbled. "Must sell the beastly pearls before I'm caught."

Jack's heart skipped several beats, and he stood transfixed. Was it possible? Could the hooded Mr. Ponji actually be Mick Muxlow?

Mr. Ponji stirred and sat upright, staring at Jack.

"What are you doing here?" he demanded.

"Forgot my apron," Jack replied. For a moment he considered pouncing upon Mr. Ponji and snatching the hood from his head, but good breeding forbade such a display of ill manners.

"I say," Jack said, struck suddenly by inspiration, "did you hear the commotion in the street a few minutes ago? Seems some fellow has stolen some valuable pearls."

"Clever," Mr. Ponji observed.

"Stupid," Jack replied.

"Stupid?" Mr. Ponji echoed.

Jack nodded.

"The thief is a chap called Muxlow and, quite between us, he is mad as a hatter."

"What a wretched thing to say!" Mr. Ponji cried.

"Nevertheless," Jack said carelessly, "it is true." He tapped his forehead. "The bird hasn't a single brain in the old onion, don't you know."

"That isn't true," Mr. Ponji cried passionately, leaping up from the bed and confronting Jack.

"How would you know?" Jack asked slyly.

Mr. Ponji threw back the hood of his robe, revealing a mop of bright red hair.

"I am Mick Muxlow," he announced, "and I am the cleverest thief in the British Empire!"

Jack snatched off his own turban and dhoti.

"You!" Muxlow cried. "Jack Wookey!"

"The same!" Jack said. "I have followed you all the way from Bombay, and now I have trapped you."

"I knew that you were following me," Mick said. "I saw you at the top of that Chinese pyramid. Not a brain in the old onion, eh? Well you're wrong. I knew the instant I saw you that you were chasing me in order to recover the pearls and make up for what you had done on the *Begum of Bengal*. Am I correct?"

Jack nodded.

"You are correct," he said. "Now I will thank you to hand over those pearls so that I can be on my way to the Queen with them."

Muxlow tumbled back on the bed laughing and clutching his sides.

"Do you think it is as easy as all that?" he gasped. "Are you such a simple daisy that you believe I will hand the pearls to you without a struggle? The money I receive from the sale of the pearls will be the foundation of my fortune."

But Jack did not hear him, for he had caught sight of the pearls, spilling from a fold in Mick Muxlow's robe. Springing forward, Jack seized the necklace and fled from the room.

Down the stairs flew Jack, with Mick Muxlow in hot pursuit.

"Don't think for a moment you can get away with this beastly trick," Muxlow bellowed. "I'll track you down before you can turn those pearls over to the Queen."

The proprietor, who stood in the open doorway of the hotel, was bowled off his feet as Jack bolted from the hotel. As he picked himself up, Muxlow collided with him, knocking him down once more.

"Here," the proprietor cried, "you gave no notice that you were quitting your jobs. Come back!"

Around the corner from the hotel, a cart drawn by a bullock rattled up the dusty street. Without pausing to consider the wisdom of his action, Jack leaped into the back of the cart and concealed himself beneath some straw. Wherever that cart was going, there was one distinct advantage: Mick Muxlow was not going along with it!

Having noted that the cart was southbound, Jack hoped it was going all the way to Bombay. He fell to calculating just how long it would take to cover the distance between Delhi and Bombay, given the snail's pace at which the cart was traveling. After some hours, Jack peeped from beneath the straw and discovered that night had come. He could discern nothing in the darkness but a sprinkling of stars overhead. Nestling down in the straw once more, he was asleep in only a moment.

But next morning when he again peeped from beneath the straw, Jack was startled to see mountains looming around him. It was obvious that somewhere along the route the cart had turned toward the north.

"Oh, dash it!" Jack muttered. "This is a piece of bad luck. I had hoped to reach Bombay quickly. The Queen will arrive in a week's time. Now what will I do?"

Jack decided to emerge from the straw and consult with the driver, in the hope that he might be persuaded to alter the course of the vehicle.

"I say," Jack called, rising and brushing the straw from his clothing, "wait up a moment while I settle on the seat beside you."

40

The driver whirled around and uttered a startled cry.
Then he breathed a deep sigh.

"At last we are alone," he said. "I've been wanting to
talk with you."

"You have?" Jack asked uncertainly. He was sure that
until a minute before the driver had not known of his
presence in the cart.

"Yes," the driver said firmly.

Jack settled himself on the seat beside the man.

"Have I ever told you about my brother Guru?"

"No," Jack said uneasily. He was on the verge of reminding the man that they had met for the first time only a few minutes before, but he wasn't certain that would be wise.

"My brother Guru," the driver continued, "is in the theater."

"That's most awfully jolly," Jack murmured politely.

The driver scowled fiercely at Jack.

"I meant to say most awfully frightful," Jack amended weakly.

The driver nodded, apparently satisfied. For several minutes he was silent.

"What was it you wanted to speak with me about?" he asked at last.

"I?" Jack asked in surprise. "But you said that you wanted to talk with me."

"Yes" the driver murmured, "of course. This entire business has upset me so that I am in a state of confusion. You understand."

Jack shook his head.

"I'm afraid I don't," he admitted. "Thus far all I am certain of is that you have a brother called Guru and that he is in the theater. I also gather that this does not altogether please you."

"You are correct!" the driver cried spiritedly. "I would not object to his choice of professions, were it not for the fact that he involves me in his work. At this very moment I am on my way to the summer home of Colonel Frobisher of the British army. The British Resident from Bombay,

Lord Lummox, is a guest there. I shall be required to take part in a theatrical performance staged by Guru. Whenever one of his players falls ill, Guru calls upon me, pleading that he will be ruined if I do not fly to his aid."

The driver threw up his hands in a gesture of helplessness.

Jack groaned. He had no desire to encounter Lord Lummox.

"How long will you remain in the mountains?" Jack asked.

"Only until tomorrow night," the driver declared firmly. "I will not be detained longer. Tonight a rehearsal will be held, and tomorrow evening the performance will take place. Then I shall return to Delhi, where I am the proprietor of a prosperous tailoring shop."

Jack thought about that. By the following evening his trail would certainly be so cold that Mick Muxlow would be unable to follow him. Then he would return to the city with the driver of the cart and begin to work his way south to Bombay. The plan was foolproof. Jack smiled and fingered the pearls inside his pocket.

"I wonder if you would drive for a while so that I might sleep," the driver suggested. "I have driven all night and I am exceedingly tired."

He retired to the straw in the back of the cart and Jack took the reins. A lesser young man than Jack might have seized the opportunity to swing the cart round and head south. But such a dishonorable thought did not enter the mind of the virtuous tar. He drove along in silence, contemplating the beauty of the day.

At sundown two events occurred simultaneously. The driver awoke, and Jack saw before them a palatial dwelling which the driver identified as the summer home of Colonel Frobisher.

"I will take the reins now," the driver said, climbing onto the seat.

Jack, remembering the scene at the Empire Hotel, decided to remain out of sight until the theatrical performance was ended and they were once again safely on the road. He convinced the driver to aid him in his plan by acquainting him with recent events.

"You may rely upon my help," the driver assured Jack. "I am sorry to hear of your misfortune. I am familiar with adversity, due to my brother Guru. I suggest you remain concealed in the straw of the cart, and I will bring you food when I am able."

"This is extremely good of you," Jack said warmly. He submerged and drew a layer of straw over his head as the cart drew up to the gates of the great house.

"Gupta," a voice called, as the gates clanged open, "I have been waiting for you. The rehearsal is about to commence."

Jack realized that the voice must be that of Guru, and that he was addressing the driver of the cart, whose name was apparently Gupta. Jack nestled deeper in the straw and listened. Guru had joined Gupta on the seat of the cart.

"What role am I to portray?" Gupta asked morosely.

"The role of the palace guard," Guru answered.

"Why am I never allowed to be the prince?" Gupta demanded petulantly.

There was no reply, but Jack felt the cart moving once more. For several minutes it rumbled along, then stopped.

"The servants will take charge of your bullock," Guru said. "We must hurry to the ballroom, where rehearsal is to be held."

"I will bring you food as soon as possible," Gupta hissed to the pile of straw.

"To whom are you speaking?" Guru demanded. "No one is there. I believe that the tailoring business has unhinged your mind. You would be wise to make the theater your profession."

As he lay in the straw, Jack heard the servants come and unharness the bullock. They laughed and chattered excitedly about the theatrical performance, which they would be permitted to witness. Then there was silence. Jack began to realize how hungry he was and he wished with all his heart that Gupta would return with food. But hours passed and still Gupta did not come back to the cart.

Peering from beneath the straw, Jack saw that the great house lay in total darkness. Obviously, everyone had gone to bed and Gupta had forgotten him. There was only one thing to be done. He, Jack, must provide his own dinner by slipping into the pantry and requisitioning supplies.

"How monstrous to realize I must actually pinch something," Jack sighed, "but there seems no other way. As soon as I am able, I must repay what I borrow."

He emerged from the straw and climbed down off the cart, straining his eyes to see in the darkness. Somehow he must find the pantry without straying into the servants' quarters, for he shuddered to imagine the scene that would ensue should he be discovered in the house.

In only a moment he had covered the distance between the cart and the house and crouched by a door which, he knew, would not be the main entrance to the house. It was, he decided, a service entrance. If that were the case it would open upon the kitchen and pantry area. Feeling confident, Jack tried the door and found it unlocked. He slipped inside and closed the door softly behind him. Advancing by a series of noiseless wiggles, he edged along a wall until he came to another door. This he opened cautiously, then stepped inside. Feeling with his hands along the wall, he discovered shelves. The room was, as he had hoped, the pantry.

After passing over tins of food, he located a cheese and some sausages. Those he stuffed inside his uniform. Then he began to search for some biscuits. But in the darkness he bumped against a rack of pots and cutlery, knocking it to the floor. The din was deafening. Jack sprang back in alarm and bolted for the door. But the door did not seem to be where he had left it. Around and around he sprinted, thumping on the walls in a vain search for the exit.

"Who's there?" a voice boomed. "Who's down there?"

Jack froze in his tracks.

46

The lights of several lamps illumined the darkness, and Jack saw, too late, the door through which he had entered the pantry. He heard the sound of hurrying footsteps and felt doom descending upon him.

But as the lamps came closer, Jack saw another door leading from the pantry. He had no notion what lay on the other side of that door, but he was in no position to be selective. He opened it quickly and edged through, closing it softly behind him. As he crouched in the darkness, he heard the party of searchers enter the pantry. The light from their lamps filtered under the door, and Jack saw that the room that he had entered was lined with racks of clothing and shelves holding what appeared to be hats. He had stumbled, he supposed, into somebody's closet or dressing room.

"There's no one here," a voice from the pantry said. "But someone has been here."

"Probably a mouse," another voice suggested.

"There were seventeen cheeses here," the first voice said, "and twelve sausages. One cheese and three sausages are missing."

"I call such efficiency devilish inconsiderate," Jack mumbled. "That man must be a positive miser to know to the very sausage what's in the pantry."

"What is the trouble here?" a new voice boomed.

Jack's heart tried unsuccessfully to leap out of his mouth. The new voice could only belong to Lord Lummox, he was certain.

"Someone was in the pantry," the first voice said. "I wonder that you didn't hear all the racket when these pots were knocked over."

"Well, why are you all standing about chatting?" Lord Lummox cried. "Let's be after the bounder. He can't have gone far."

Jack whimpered softly to himself.

"Here now," he whispered sternly, "this won't do. A British tar is resourceful. There must be some way to squirm out of this mess."

Looking around for another door, he noticed once more the clothing that hung on the surrounding racks.

That's it, he thought. But how will I explain my presence?

He seized the nearest garment, a long and fashionable silk bombazine gown, and wriggled into it.

"I'll worry about an explanation later," he muttered. "Some idea will probably suggest itself."

Groping along one of the shelves, his hand came upon something soft and hairy. He nearly whooped aloud with delight.

"A wig," he whispered delightedly. "This room must be the repository for theatrical costumes that Guru's company uses."

He clapped the wig upon his head and, finding a bonnet, placed it atop the wig and tied its ribbons beneath his chin.

He had finished not a moment too soon. The door from the pantry swung wide, revealing Lord Lummox holding a lamp in his hand. Behind him and peering around his enormous bulk, the faces of servants could be seen.

"Ah ha! you blighter!" Lord Lummox cried.

Then the light of the lamp shone full upon Jack. The

skirt of his silk dress fell in soft folds and his curls tumbled winsomely over his shoulders. The plume in his bonnet still trembled from the haste with which the hat had been donned.

"Madam!" Lord Lummox cried. "I beg your pardon. We thought you were a sneak thief."

Jack tittered nervously.

"Little old me?" he giggled. "Fancy that."

A tall, distinguished gentleman, clad in a bathrobe, edged around Lord Lummox.

"I am Colonel Frobisher, madam," he said. "You are the new governess?"

"I am?" Jack gulped. "Oh, I am, I am!"

"What are you doing here, in the middle of the night?" Lord Lummox demanded.

"Probably came up from Delhi with that theatrical chap's brother," Colonel Frobisher said. "Isn't that right?"

Jack nodded mutely. Decidedly considerate of Frobisher to provide all the answers.

"But where have you been?" Lord Lummox persisted. "That cart arrived hours ago."

Jack thought fast.

"I was walking in the garden," he said, pitching his voice as high as he was able. "It was so lovely that I lost track of time. I tried to enter the house without disturbing anyone, but unfortunately I was not able to do so."

"Higglesford will show you to your room," Frobisher said. "Miss Goodle, isn't it?"

Jack nodded vigorously, his curls bobbing.

"Miss Goodle it is," he confirmed.

"Mrs. Frobisher and the children have not yet arrived home from their holiday in England," the Colonel said, "but we will endeavor to make you comfortable. We have planned a little theatrical for tomorrow evening in honor of Lord Lummox here."

Lord Lummox bowed gallantly by way of introduction and Jack did his best at a curtsy. It was none too graceful.

"Let's all get some sleep now," Colonel Frobisher suggested. "All this excitement has been jolly, but we want to be fresh in the morning, what?"

The entire company trooped upstairs and Jack, led by Higglesford, entered a large and comfortably furnished room.

"Madam has no luggage?" Higglesford asked.

"Simply tons of it," Jack replied in a high voice, "but it was stolen from me in Delhi. Thoughtless, I call it."

"Oh, indeed," Higglesford agreed.

When Higglesford had gone, Jack bolted the door and breathed a deep sigh. Then he removed the long gown, bonnet, and wig and stretched out upon the bed. He devoured the cheese and sausages, and in only a few minutes he was asleep.

Next morning Jack arose and dressed once more in the costume of the night before. He peered anxiously into the glass above the wardrobe, wondering whether the disguise would be as successful in the broad light of day as it had been by lamplight.

"I'll have to risk it," he murmured aloud.

Unbolting the door, he started down the wide curving staircase. But his pace was too rapid, and the full skirt of the long bombazine gown whipped about his legs until it tripped him and sent him tumbling head first to the floor below. He sat up, dazed, his bonnet askew atop his curls.

"Miss Goodle!" Lord Lummox cried. "What a frightful accident. Are you all right?"

Jack climbed to his feet and staggered about in a small circle, rubbing his head.

"I'm not sure," Jack moaned, forgetting for a moment to lift his voice to a higher register.

But Lord Lummox did not seem to notice, for he dashed away and returned in a few seconds carrying a large overstuffed chair. Placing it at the foot of the stairs, he assisted Jack to it, guiding him gently. Then he dashed away again, returning with an embroidered Spanish fan, which he began to ply vigorously to and fro. Jack steadied his bonnet and hoped devoutly that it would not be dislodged from his head, along with his wig.

"What has happened?" Colonel Frobisher cried, coming upon the scene.

"Miss Goodle has taken a nasty fall," Lord Lummox re-

plied, doubling the speed with which he wielded the fan.

"This is a fair gale," Jack mumbled.

"Beg pardon?" Lord Lummox said.

"I said I am doubtless very pale," Jack replied hastily. Both men nodded.

"What you want is a bit of air," Colonel Frobisher declared. "We will take you to the garden. The theatrical company is there, soaking up a bit of sun. You know the tailor, Gupta, of course, and you might enjoy chatting with him."

Jack swallowed hard. Would Gupta recognize him beneath the disguise? And if he did, would he cry out in surprise, giving the secret away? And what of the other members of the company? It was entirely possible that someone would recognize the silk dress and bonnet he was wearing.

But it was too late to protest, for Lord Lummox and Colonel Frobisher had already grasped Jack firmly by the

52

elbows and were propelling him through the large French doors into the garden.

Members of the theatrical company strolled about the garden, among the roses and delphiniums. Jack saw Gupta and noted the preoccupied expression on the tailor's face. Jack surmised that Gupta had taken food to the cart and found him gone. He was probably wondering what had become of his stowaway.

"There you are!" Colonel Frobisher called, addressing Gupta. "Miss Goodle has had a bit of an accident and wants a bit of air. Do come and sit with her for a while."

Gupta seemed genuinely puzzled.

"Miss Goodle?" he asked, coming to the bench where Jack now sat and peering into Jack's face.

"Yes," Lord Lummox snapped impatiently, "Miss Goodle. The woman you brought with you from Delhi yesterday."

Gupta's eyes grew wide, but he said nothing. He sank

53

down upon the bench beside Jack.

Apparently satisfied, Lord Lummox and Colonel Frobisher left the garden and returned to the house. Jack thought, as they walked away, that he heard the name Mick Muxlow, but he could not be sure.

"Is it you?" Gupta whispered, peering once again into Jack's face.

"Yes," Jack said softly, "it is. And I thank you for not giving me away. When you didn't come with food for me last night, I slipped into the pantry and pinched some cheese and sausages. Unfortunately I knocked over a rack of pots and aroused the entire household. I wonder that you didn't hear the commotion."

"Our quarters are in the west wing of the house," Gupta said, "and that is a great distance from the pantry and kitchen. But how did you come to adopt the disguise of Miss Goodle?"

Jack related the events of the night before and Gupta listened quietly.

"I do not believe Guru will recognize that costume," he said, when Jack had finished. "The stock of dresses and robes and headgear that he carries with him is so great that he could not possibly recall them all. Now, my advice to you is to maintain this disguise until tonight's performance is ended. At that time I shall smuggle you into the cart once more, and we shall be off to Delhi."

"I shall give it a go," Jack said. "It's sporting of you to help me. I shall meet you here in the garden as soon as the performance is done and we will go to the cart together."

Jack rose, bade Gupta goodbye, and minced toward the

house, careful this time that his long skirt did not trip him. As he stepped through the French doors, the voices of Lord Lummox and Colonel Frobisher drifted to him from the study.

"Only one week until Her Majesty arrives in Bombay," Lord Lummox moaned. "Have you come up with any clues as to the whereabouts of Muxlow?"

"None at all," Frobisher admitted grimly. "But see here, old man, we mustn't give up. Who can tell what might happen in a week's time?"

"Who indeed?" Jack murmured, gliding past the study door and up the stairs to the privacy of his room.

Pleading a headache, Jack succeeded in persuading Higglesford to serve luncheon on a tray so that he would not need to risk the company of Lord Lummox and Colonel Frobisher. It was growing increasingly difficult for Jack to maintain the high voice with which he had invested the character of Miss Goodle.

Following luncheon, Jack rested, plotting his journey south from Delhi, until evening came and dinner was announced.

"Ah, the festive board!" Colonel Frobisher cried expansively, as he entered the dining room. "And afterward we shall all gather in the ballroom and see what delights Guru has in store for us. Cheer up, Lummox old thing. Don't look so downhearted."

But Lord Lummox did not cheer up. Indeed, so woebegone was his expression as he contemplated the missing pearls and the imminent arrival of his sovereign that

Jack feared he would weep into the soup. The meal was a quiet affair, with every attempt at conversation on Frobisher's part met with silence.

At length dinner was finished, and Jack and Lord Lummox followed the Colonel into the ballroom. They settled themselves in comfortable chairs and the Colonel signaled that the entertainment might commence.

But no sooner had the curtain been rung up on a scene of courtly splendor, in which Guru portrayed an emperor of Japan, than a raucous voice from the garden broke the spell of enchantment.

"Fortunes!" the voice bellowed. "Learn what fate holds in store for you. Old Tootie sees all."

"*Awp*," Jack cried, shooting some twelve inches straight up from his chair.

"Who is there, Higglesford?" Colonel Frobisher called. "Who is that shouting?"

Higglesford bustled into the ballroom.

56

"It is some gypsy person, sir," he explained. "She will not go away, but insists upon coming in here."

"Stand aside," Tootie cried, striding into the ballroom. "I am here to reveal the future to one and all."

"See here, madam," Lord Lummox roared, rising from his chair, "what does this mean?"

Tootie shook her head sadly.

"You're not paying attention," she said severely. "Now listen. I have come to tell your fortunes. I learned that festivities were in order here tonight and, being a girl with an eye to the main chance, I saw the possibility of picking up a bit of small change and at the same time doing good by reading your futures."

Higglesford, who had retired from the ballroom when Tootie made her way in, now returned, escorting a gentleman swathed in a large hooded robe. If Jack had leaped, astonished, from his chair at the arrival of the gypsy, that was as nothing compared to his performance when he beheld the hooded man, whom he recognized at once as Mick Muxlow in the disguise of Mr. Ponji.

"I say," Lord Lummox cried, falling to his knees before Jack's chair and fanning the young man briskly with a slender volume of sonnets, which had lain on a table nearby. "I fear Miss Goodle has suffered an attack of some sort!"

Jack lay back in his chair, a stricken expression on his face. He was perspiring profusely, and from time to time he uttered a strangled gasp not unlike the sound that the boat train to Harwich makes when easing into the station.

"Not surprising," Colonel Frobisher said, pouring water from a decanter into a glass and pressing it insistently to Jack's lips, "what with all this excitement."

He turned to Higglesford.

"Who is this man?" he demanded, indicating Mr. Ponji.

"He came along with me," Tootie announced. "His name is Mr. Ponji and he has business in these regions. He was grateful for the ride in my cart."

Lord Lummox stopped fanning Jack and resumed his own chair.

"It occurs to me," he said, "that we would all be grateful for some order and tranquillity. Frobisher, let us enjoy the entertainment and then permit this gypsy to tell our fortunes. While I do not put faith in such superstitions, it will nonetheless be entertaining."

Colonel Frobisher signaled for the entertainment to proceed, and Guru's company, which had watched the scene in the ballroom with much interest, commenced the play.

Tootie settled herself in a chair beside Jack's while Mr.

58

Ponji crouched in the corner of a sofa, surveying the scene with puzzled frown.

"What are you doing here?" Jack hissed.

"Beg pardon, madam," Tootie rasped, "but I explained all that."

Jack seized the gypsy by the sleeve of her robe and drew her close to him.

"I know what you said," he insisted, "but what I want to know is what you are really doing here!"

"Is that you?" Tootie cried, peering closely at Jack's face.

Jack clapped a hand across her mouth.

"Shhh," Lord Lummox whispered, raising a finger to his lips.

"It's I, all right," Jack confirmed. "Now answer my question. You may just possibly have ruined my entire life by coming here, and I want to know what the great big idea is."

Tootie scowled.

"Ruined your life?" she echoed. "You asked me to help you, and I could not help you when I didn't even know where you were. When you didn't come to my shop as we had planned, I went to your hotel and learned that you had left suddenly without leaving a forwarding address. Mr. Ponji had only just come into the hotel after searching for you, and he offered to assist me in locating you. Fortunately, Abu, the sugar merchant, saw you enter Gupta's cart and he knew where Gupta was going. It seems Mr. Ponji has a message for you."

Jack clapped a hand to his brow.

"He has a message for me, right enough," he said. "He

wants to tell me that he has come to pinch the pearls from me. Mr. Ponji, for your enlightenment, is Mick Muxlow in disguise. I found him out at the hotel, snatched the pearls from him, and fled. Now you have delivered him to my doorstep!"

Tootie gasped.

"I didn't know!" she said. "I didn't recognize him. Do you think he has recognized you?"

Jack shrugged and looked warily toward where Mick Muxlow sat. Their eyes met and for a moment a flicker of recognition seemed to dawn on Muxlow's face.

"I think he's getting a glimmer," Jack said. "But he won't dare make his move here. Lord Lummox and Colonel Frobisher would nab him."

"On the other hand," Tootie observed, "you do not dare make a move or you will be caught and lose the pearls. Is it still your plan to present them to the Queen?"

"It is," Jack said, "although at this moment my chances for doing so seem to be growing slighter and slighter."

They fell silent, Jack peeping furtively from time to time at Mick Muxlow. All the while, his brain was working furiously, planning an escape that would put the greatest possible time and distance between Muxlow and himself.

At length the entertainment was finished, and Guru came forth to receive the accolades of the audience, followed by his entire company. Gupta was there in his costume, and Jack tried unsuccessfully to catch his eye. Then the performers retired to the improvised dressing room, and Tootie prepared to tell the fortunes of Lord Lummox and Colonel Frobisher.

"Ah," the gypsy cried, gazing at Lummox's outstretched palm, "I see that you are greatly troubled."

Lord Lummox groaned.

"I had nearly forgotten," he said. "The performance was so diverting that the matter of the pearls slipped from my mind."

"I can tell without even looking at your palm," Tootie said, addressing Colonel Frobisher, "that you are involved in the same difficulty that troubles this gentleman."

"Extraordinary!" Frobisher muttered. "Jolly clever of you."

"Heed the gypsy's advice," Tootie warned. "You must seek the wisdom of the East. I suggest that you go to Mr. Ponji and confide your problem to him. Take him into a quiet corner, away from the hurly-burly, and insist that he remain with you for a lengthy conversation."

Jack understood what Tootie was doing. She was buying him time in which to make his escape by seeing to it that Mick Muxlow was kept busy. Good old gypsy.

"Capital plan!" Lord Lummox cried. "Mysterious East, wisdom of the ages and all that, what?"

. He leaped to his feet and hastened to where Mr. Ponji sat, desperate for any help in recovering the missing pearls.

"Stout fellow, Ponji," he said. "Come along, Frobisher, and let us seek wisdom from this oracle!"

Mick Muxlow cast one last long suspicious look over his shoulder at Jack as he was borne away. Jack was nearly certain that Muxlow had guessed it was he, Jack, lurking beneath the curls and gown.

Now what do you think of my gypsy powers?"
Tootie gloated, turning to Jack.

"You were magnificent!" Jack cried, pumping her hand vigorously up and down. "Now I shall make my escape!"

The gypsy raised a hand to silence him.

"I will manage things," she said haughtily. "I shall take complete charge of matters and see that you reach Bombay with the pearls in time to greet the Queen."

"You needn't—" Jack began.

"Tut, tut!" Tootie said arrogantly. "Have no fear. Just do as I say and all will be well."

"Very well," Jack said, impressed by her confidence. "You did handle the matter of Muxlow with efficiency."

"Now tell me," Tootie said, "the manner in which you planned to leave this place."

Jack told her of his plan to meet Gupta in the garden and steal away with him in the darkness. At that very moment, he supposed, Gupta must be awaiting him among the delphiniums.

"Here is what you must do," Tootie said. "You must remove that gown and wig and bonnet and don another of Guru's costumes. When Muxlow finally manages to slip away from Lord Lummox and Colonel Frobisher, he will come after you, and of course he would recognize you in that disguise. I am almost certain he saw through it as he was being led away."

Jack nodded his agreement.

"I will go and find another disguise for you," Tootie said. "Where can you go to change into it?"

Jack told her what room had been assigned to Miss Goodle; then he went there to await her. So anxious was he to be away from the house that as he ascended the stairs he untied the ribbons of his bonnet and took it off. In his haste he failed to notice that the wig had slipped from his head and fallen upon the stairs.

The gypsy arrived in only a few minutes, bearing a Japanese kimono and another wig, a glossy black one. Jack donned them hurriedly.

"All clear," Tootie announced, peering into the corridor. "Have you the pearls?"

"I have them," Jack said. "Now let's get out of here quickly."

But before they had reached the foot of the stairs Lord Lummox and Colonel Frobisher emerged from the study, followed by Mr. Ponji.

"Frightfully strange fellow," Frobisher muttered. "Wouldn't utter a single word." Then he saw Jack and the gypsy descending the stairs.

"You there, gypsy," he cried, "what are you doing there? Who is that with you?"

Lord Lummox, catching sight of something lying upon the stairs, charged forward and scooped it up in his great hands. It was the wig that Jack had worn as Miss Goodle. He uttered a strangled cry.

"What have you done with Miss Goodle, you fiends?" he roared, turning with savage fury upon Jack and the gypsy.

Colonel Frobisher, clearly a man of action, burst past them and up the stairs to Miss Goodle's room. Seizing the opportunity, Jack and Tootie fled through the French doors and into the garden, followed by the others in the following order:

1. Lord Lummox—Who believed some ghastly crime had been perpetrated
2. Mick Muxlow—Who had deduced at once what was taking place
3. Higglesford—Who held Lord Lummox's overcoat and beseeched him to beware the night air
4. Colonel Frobisher—A late arrival, determined not to be excluded from the proceedings

"Look what you have done," Jack panted, as he and Tootie circled a bed of lavender. "You demanded to be placed in charge, and you have made a perfect mess of things!"

"You ought to have restrained me," Tootie whimpered. "I am only a woman and could not be expected to manage such a complicated affair. It's all your fault for having permitted me to take charge!"

As the group rounded a tall hedge for the fourth time, Jack thought he perceived in the shadows another, darker, shape.

"Gupta," Jack hissed, "is that you?"

The dark shape leaned out from the shrubbery and peered at Jack.

"It is I," the shape confirmed. "Who are you, and what is happening here?"

"No time for explanations now," Jack cried. "Take us to your cart."

Gupta shook his head firmly.

"My cart is reserved for another," he explained. "I will not leave without him."

At that point, Jack and Tootie were forced to leave Gupta and circle the hedge, for their pursuers had nearly caught up with them. But, next time around, Jack hurriedly explained the change of costume to Gupta, and the three dashed to the waiting cart.

"I wonder if they will follow us," Tootie mused, as the cart rumbled down the road by the light of a full moon.

"Undoubtedly," Jack said. "Lord Lummox and Colonel Frobisher are certain to see that the wig was only a wig after all, and that the gown and bonnet were part of a disguise. They will want to know who Miss Goodle really was. Mick Muxlow, alias Mr. Ponji, knows very well who I am, and he will make one final attempt to gain possession of the pearls before I hand them to the Queen. I am in trouble."

Tootie sniffed disdainfully.

"You have been in trouble all along," she observed. "And now I have lost a perfectly good cart, having left it behind, and I am in trouble for helping you. I could be taken to court for having assisted a fugitive from justice, since I know you are in possession of stolen goods. They would say I should have turned you over to Lord Lummox back there at the house."

"But you didn't," Jack said warmly, "and I won't forget your friendship. Or yours either, Gupta."

Jack settled down in the straw at the back of the cart to sleep, leaving Tootie and Gupta to talk as the cart jolted along.

Dawn came, and the travelers were still some distance from Delhi. Jack realized with a start that only five days now remained before the Queen's ship would dock in Bombay. He meant to put those pearls in her hands before any further complications ensued.

Back in Delhi once more, Jack bade farewell to Gupta.

"I wish I could help you further," Gupta said, "but I have my tailoring business to care for. Any day Guru may send another urgent message and I will be off to Calcutta or even Hong Kong to portray a streetsweeper or onion merchant. My best wishes go with you, however."

"I will go with you to Bombay," Tootie assured Jack.

"Oh," Jack cried hastily, "that isn't at all necessary. I'm

sure I can manage without help. Of course I appreciate your offer."

"I will go with you," Tootie said firmly. "My gypsy powers tell me that more trouble lies ahead of you, and I won't desert you now."

Jack sighed.

"You need no gypsy powers to foresee that more trouble lies ahead," he said. "You need merely to know my history and the situation I am presently involved in. Come along if you like."

Before leaving Delhi for Bombay, Jack shed the Japanese robe and wig that he had donned at Colonel Frobisher's home. The disguise was useless, since Muxlow had seen him in it, and since Lord Lummox and the Colonel would be on the lookout for a Japanese gentleman. He decided to risk proceeding the remainder of the way in his British uniform, hoping Muxlow would not come near enough to recognize him.

The journey to Bombay took four days and four nights, and when Jack and Tootie arrived there, they found the city in the grip of panic. The necklace of black pearls had, of course, not yet been recovered and British authorities had redoubled their efforts to locate the jewels.

"There is not a place in all Bombay that would be safe from search," Tootie said glumly.

"There is one place," Jack said, smiling slyly. "Tell me, how do you feel about closets?"

"Closets?" the gypsy echoed uncertainly. "I confess I have given them little consideration."

Jack motioned for her to come nearer so that he might whisper a plan to her.

"Suppose," he said, "we went to the British Government House——"

"What?" Tootie shrieked.

Jack clapped a hand to her mouth hastily.

"Hear me out," he whispered. "Suppose, by clever means, we enter the house unseen and secret ourselves in a closet, remaining there until the Queen arrives tomorrow. The Government House is one place which will not be searched, and we will be safe. Muxlow will not find us there either."

"This is madness!" the gypsy groaned.

Jack smiled happily.

"Yes, it is rather," he agreed. "But I believe it will work. Shall we give it a go?"

Having agreed, the two set off at once and reached the Government House just at dusk. The sun had gone down, but the lamps inside the building had not yet been lit. Jack, followed closely by Tootie, slipped through the open gates at the front of the house, bolted across the open yard, and slid around to the rear of the building. There the two cowered, listening for the sound of running feet, a guard's whistle, or other signs that would indicate they had been observed. There was only silence. Feeling quite confident, Jack tried a window and found it unlocked. It was the work of only a moment to climb through the window and pull the gypsy in after him.

"Now to locate a nice cozy closet," Jack whispered. "There ought to be one nearby."

"There must be a mop and broom closet," Tootie ventured. "It would be here at the rear of the building."

"Good thinking!" Jack whispered. "Let's have a look."

Creeping down a passageway, they found the mop and broom closet immediately next to the service entrance. They slipped inside and pulled the door nearly shut, leaving just a crack through which to breathe.

"Stuffy," Jack murmured, disentangling himself from a cluster of mops.

"Smells of oil and lampblack," Tootie said, sniffing.

"We will be able to withstand the discomfort until tomorrow," Jack said. "I only hope no one comes to remove a broom or a mop and finds us hiding here."

The lights in the house were lit at last, and dinner was prepared. Jack and Tootie heard the clink of china and silver as the table in the dining room was laid for the meal. They heard, too, the voice of Lord Lummox and knew he had returned from the north to conduct the ceremonies of the following day.

"He must be very upset because the pearls have not been recovered," Jack mused, fingering the necklace in his pocket. "I wonder what he would say if he knew those pearls were in his own mop closet at this very moment."

At last the house was quiet, and Jack and Tootie sank to the floor and fell asleep in a cramped position, their heads pillowed on the shaggy mops.

Next morning Jack was awakened by the aroma of sausages and coffee. He crouched there with his eyes closed for a few minutes, picturing the breakfast that must be spread before Lord Lummox. Then he nudged Tootie to awaken her.

"We won't have long to wait now," he whispered. "The Queen's ship is probably in port, and she will disembark immediately after breakfast. That's the way those things are done, I have heard."

"Speaking of breakfast—" Tootie said.

"I know how you are feeling," Jack replied. "I'm hungry too. But we must remain here until the moment comes to present the pearls."

For a time after the aromas of breakfast had vanished, all was quiet. Jack surmised that Lord Lummox had gone to welcome the Queen ashore. He fumbled nervously with the pearls, wishing that they were in the hands of Her Majesty and that his own honor had been restored.

Then a hum of voices broke the stillness.

"The Queen must have arrived," Tootie whispered. "Let's get out of this closet, give her the necklace, and find a few lonely little sausages that need comforting."

"All in good time," Jack said softly. "I want to make sure she is out there before I go barging in and fall into the clutches of Lord Lummox."

He pressed his ear to the closet door and listened attentively.

"Candles!" a voice boomed.

"Who was that?" Tootie asked. "Where did that voice come from?"

"I don't know," Jack whispered.

"Candles for sale!" the voice cried again.

Jack scowled.

70

"I know that voice," he muttered, "but I can't think who ——"

Jack and Tootie heard hurrying footsteps; then a door near the closet creaked open.

"What do you want here?" a woman's voice asked.

"I am a poor peddler," a voice replied, "and I have candles for sale."

"You shouldn't have come here," the woman said severely. "Her Majesty the Queen is in the parlor at this very moment. We have no time to spare for peddlers today."

"Candles!" the peddler roared. "Buy my candles!"

Tootie nudged Jack sharply in the ribs.

"I've heard that voice before too," she said. "But I can't remember where."

"Do stop howling," the woman at the door snapped. "I will purchase some of your candles. Bring them in and put them in that mop closet while I go and get some money. Then you must be on your way."

Footsteps sounded outside the closet, then the door was opened wide. Light flooded in, revealing Jack and Tootie, huddled against the brooms and mops.

"Mr. Ponji!" Tootie squealed.

"You mean Mick Muxlow!" Jack cried.

"Ah ha!" Mick Muxlow sneered. "I have found you. I didn't think it would prove so simple. I planned to gain entrance to the house and catch you just as you were about to give the pearls to the Queen."

Jack burst suddenly past Mick Muxlow and dashed down the passageway. He took the pearls from his pocket and waved them as though they were a banner of victory.

"I'm going to give them to her now," he shouted over his shoulder, "and you can't stop me, old thing."

He raced on, Muxlow in pursuit. Suddenly the pearls were swept from Jack's hand by a low-hanging drapery. In a flash, Mick Muxlow swooped up the necklace and dashed away in the opposite direction. Jack slid to a halt, turned around and charged after him.

"I have him cornered!" Tootie cried, flying at Muxlow from the other end of the passageway.

"No such thing!" Muxlow jeered, altering his course and darting through a nearby doorway.

The doorway opened into the parlor, where the Queen, flanked by Lord Lummox and Pippin-Fry, were greeting dignitaries.

Straight through the room raced Muxlow, with Jack galloping after him.

"See here—" Lord Lummox bellowed, as the two men disappeared out another doorway and up the stairs.

"I say," Pippin-Fry mumbled, "those chaps aren't on the guest list."

72

Tootie burst through the parlor, upsetting a tea tray.

"Those persons must be stopped!" Lord Lummox roared.

"Quite so," Pippin-Fry said heartily. "How do you propose to do it?"

"I," Lord Lummox thundered, "do not propose to do it! You must do it. They are mad!"

Muxlow, muddled concerning the whereabouts of the door he had entered the house by, shot down the back stairs and through the parlor once more. Jack was hard in pursuit, and Tootie labored after them, bawling encouragement to Jack.

"After them, Pippin-Fry!" Lord Lummox shouted.

Pippin-Fry raced off, leaving Lord Lummox to minister to the Queen and the visiting dignitaries, who seemed nearly overcome with shock.

In only a few moments Mick Muxlow chugged into the parlor for the third time, clearly out of breath. As he reached the place where a maid was cleaning up the fallen tea tray and cups, Jack, hard on his heels, lunged and snatched the hooded robe from his shoulders. Then the two of them slipped on a pool of cream and fell in a tangled heap at the feet of the Queen.

In one short moment Tootie and Pippin-Fry, dashing heedlessly through the room, had joined the jumble on the floor.

"Mick Muxlow!" Lord Lummox shrieked, pointing with a long finger. "Pippin-Fry, seize that man!"

Pippin-Fry struggled to his feet and clapped a hand on

Mick Muxlow's collar.

"You're under arrest," he said severely. "Where are the pearls?"

"Here they are!" Jack shouted, snatching the necklace from Muxlow's grasp.

Jack helped Tootie to her feet, and the two of them stood blushing before the Queen. Mick Muxlow was hauled unceremoniously away, and the Queen motioned for Jack and the gypsy to be seated.

"I would be most interested to hear how all of this came about," she said graciously.

"So would I!" Lord Lummox snapped. "I distinctly told you, Wookey, to keep clear of our investigation of the theft."

Tootie drew back indignantly.

"You ought to be grateful to Jack!" she cried. "Why, if it hadn't been for him, you never would have recovered those pearls at all!"

"I've seen you someplace before," Lord Lummox said,

studying the gypsy. "It will all come back to me, I'm sure."

The Queen smiled.

"Let us hear their story," she suggested. "But first, if the young man would present me with the pearls, I would be delighted to receive them."

Jack rose and bowed. Then, with a trembling hand, he presented the necklace to the Queen.

When they had heard Jack's story, the Queen smiled, and Lord Lummox rose to his feet and applauded.

"I said it before," Lord Lummox cried, "and I will say it again, Wookey. You are a plucky chap."

"It was nothing any other British tar would not have done," Jack said modestly. "At any rate, I was once a British tar."

"And so you shall be again!" Lord Lummox said. "I shall see to it that you are restored to duty at once. Carry on."

Jack snapped proudly to attention and grinned broadly. Then he watched as Lord Lummox took a beribboned medal from his own chest and pinned it to Tootie's robe.

"This is to signify," Lord Lummox announced, "that you have given service to the Empire. We are proud of you."

Tea was served and Jack and Tootie ate hungrily. Then they left the Government House and went to stroll beside the harbor and look at the Queen's ship.

"Will you continue to steal from the poor and sell to the rich?" Jack asked, wondering if events had made an impression on the gypsy.

"No," Tootie replied, "never again. Having been to tea

with the Queen, I feel a sudden desire for respectability. There is one thing that I must do, however."

Reaching inside her robe, she brought forth Jack's gold watch and handed it solemnly to him.

"It didn't run very well anyway," she said.

■